HILLSIDE PUBLIC LIBRARY
3 1992 00201 4752
JUN 25 2014

P9-AOT-321

New Americans

By
Geoffrey C. Harrison
and
Thomas F. Scott

NorwoodHouse Press
CHICAGO, ILLINOIS

Norwood House Press
PO Box 316598
Chicago, Illinois 60631

For information regarding Norwood House Press, please visit our website at:
www.norwoodhousepress.com or call 866-565-2900.

Photo Credits:
Library of Congress (4, 9, 11, 12, 13, 16, 18, 22, 23, 28, 30, 35, 43 left & right, 44);
Associated Press (34, 36, 38, 39, 41, 45).

Cover: Ralph Freso/Associated Press (left) & Ross D. Franklin/Associated Press (right)

Edited by Mark Stewart and Mike Kennedy.
Designed by Ron Jaffe.
Special thanks to Content Consultant Kim Greene.

Library of Congress Cataloging-in-Publication Data

Harrison, Geoffrey.
New Americans / by Geoffrey C. Harrison and Thomas F. Scott ;
contributor: Mark Stewart
pages cm. -- (Great debates)
Includes bibliographical references and index.
Summary: "Informational text uses a historical framework to
discuss issues surrounding immigration. Sections include opinions
from notable Americans on various sides of the issue followed by
encouragement for readers to analyze each opinion."— Provided by the
publisher.
ISBN 978-1-59953-591-3 (library edition : alk. paper)
ISBN 978-1-60357-571-3 (ebook)
1. United States--Emigration and immigration--History--Juvenile
literature. 2. United States--Emigration and immigration--
Government
policy--Juvenile literature. I. Scott, Thomas F. II. Title.
JV6450.H358 2013
325.73--dc23

2013013010

Manufactured in the United States of America in Brainerd, Minnesota.
234N—072013

COVER: The immigration debate sparks fierce emotion on both sides.

Contents

INTRODUCTION

Note: Words that are **bolded** in the text are defined in the glossary.

INTRODUCTION

We have issues ...

History doesn't just happen. It isn't made simply with the delivery of a speech or the stroke of a pen. If you look closely at every important event in the story of America, you are likely to discover deep thinking, courageous action, powerful emotion ... and great debates.

This book explores the ongoing debate about immigration in the United States. It looks at the struggles and triumphs of "new" Americans through the major questions that have shaped their experiences. Some of the arguments you read about will be familiar—people have been making them for more than two centuries. Other issues are more recent.

Throughout our country's history, some Americans have welcomed immigrants with open arms. Others have argued that we should close our borders. This debate is largely responsible for who we are today. Indeed, everyone in the U.S. can trace his or her family history back to some kind

Immigrant families prepare to begin life in America. This photo was taken in the early 1900s at Ellis Island in New York harbor.

Join the Debate

Debate is the art of discussing a controversial topic using logic and reason. One side takes the affirmative side of an issue and the other takes the negative side. Remember, however, that a great debate does not necessarily need to be an argument—often it is a matter of opinion, with each side supporting its viewpoint with facts. The key is to gather enough information to create a strong opinion. Out in the real world, debate has fewer rules and can get noisy and ugly. But on the big issues in America, debate is often how compromises are made and things get done.

of immigrant experience. Do you know where your family's story began?

Archaeologists have found no evidence that humans reached North America prior to the last Ice Age. The continent's first inhabitants came from central Asia and are the ancestors of Native Americans. Europeans reached North America more than 1,000 years ago. They did not begin to arrive in great numbers until the 1500s. Within a few centuries, these new Americans were overwhelming the country's native inhabitants. The nation has been shaped by its newcomers ever since. The lure of open living spaces, abundant natural resources, exciting business opportunities—and freedom—convinced people to risk everything and journey to North America. After the United States won its independence from England in 1783, that draw became even stronger.

Make Your Case

In Chapter 2 through Chapter 5, you will find special sections entitled **Make Your Case**. Each one highlights different sides of the debate on immigration using quotes from prominent Americans. **Make Your Case** lets you analyze the speaker's point of view … and challenges you to form an opinion of your own. You'll find additional famous opinion-makers on the immigration debate in Chapter 7.

The bold experiment of American democracy demanded strong backs for physical labor and determined minds. The country counted on newcomers to supply these ingredients. Nevertheless, each group of immigrants has faced hardship and prejudice, often from the groups that had arrived just before them. In the end, however, they found a way to make the country their own. And in doing so, they made America.

What do the challenges and obstacles faced by new Americans say about America itself? As you will see, the debate over immigration offers a window into the character of the country, as well as into human nature. People often fear what they do not understand. Indeed, what is harder to understand than a new neighbor whose language and clothes and music and food seem completely alien? Keep this in mind as you read about these great debates.

1 Should "old" Americans decide who gets to be a "new" American?

During the early 1800s, ships loaded with immigrants began landing on the shores of the United States in great numbers. That worried Americans who didn't want to share everything they had worked for and fought for. Their philosophy, called Nativism, held that people who already live in the United States should have greater rights and freedoms than immigrants new to the country. The first great debate on immigration focused on the fairness of Nativism …

AFFIRMATIVE SIDE

Anyone willing to work hard should be rewarded with entry into America. Denying someone citizenship because of where that person comes from is the worst kind of prejudice. The U.S. needs men and women with strong backs and courageous hearts if it wants to stand as an equal with the great international powers.

John Adams, the second U.S. President, was wary of newcomers.

Who is a Native?

The inhabitants of the original 13 colonies were made up of different ethnic groups, but for the most part they came to think of themselves as being English. When the colonists were denied the benefits and freedoms enjoyed by citizens of England, they began to think of themselves as something else: *Americans*. After defeating the English in the Revolutionary War, Americans began to develop a strong national identity—and with it came a suspicion of newcomers.

In 1798, President John Adams took the first **federal** action against immigration with the Alien and Sedition Acts.

NEGATIVE SIDE

America is a young country. It struggled long and hard for its freedom. The people who joined this struggle deserve to enjoy more power and privilege than immigrants. Americans are right to be suspicious of people fleeing the hardships of Europe to enjoy the advantages for which we "natives" risked everything.

Make Your Case

"The tendency of the thing is **injurious**, unless the newcomers are more civilized and more virtuous, and have … the same ideas and feeling about government."

Samuel Whelpley, 1825

Whelpley was an author and historian—and also a Nativist. He argued that only those immigrants who measured up to American standards should be allowed into the country.

Had the U.S. placed stricter rules on immigration, what would the effect have been on important projects that relied on large amounts of manual labor?

These new laws increased the time it took immigrants to become citizens from five years to 14. They gave the government power to arrest or deport immigrants considered to be "dangerous to the peace and safety" of the country. The passage of these laws also marked the beginning of carefully recorded immigration statistics.

A Question of Religion

In the years that followed, Americans turned a suspicious eye toward other immigrant groups, particularly those who followed the Catholic faith. During the 1820s, large numbers of newcomers started arriving from Ger-

This cartoon from the mid-1800s shows a Catholic priest landing in America. At the time, many feared that members of the Catholic faith would abuse the freedoms the U.S. offered. These fears turned out to be untrue.

many and Ireland. Their labor was critical to the success of large projects being undertaken across the country. A high percentage of the German and Irish immigrants were Catholics. Many Americans believed that Catholics were faithful only to their spiritual leader in Rome, the Pope. Nativists used this **rationale** as part of their argument to keep Catholics out of the country.

By the 1850s, Nativism had become a powerful force in American politics. Most notable was the Know-Nothing Party, which worked to limit citizenship and restrict the rights of newcomers. The party was made up of middle-class American males, most of whom were **Protestant** and had descended from English colonists. The Know-Nothings and groups like them enjoyed great power for several years, and were behind much of the violence aimed at new Americans.

In 1855, the Know-Nothings supported Levi Boone for Mayor of Chicago. Boone won the election and

Make Your Case

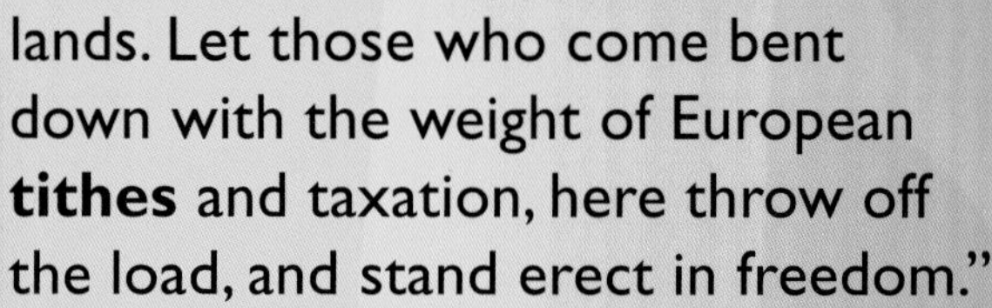

"Let our country be the asylum of the oppressed of all lands. Let those who come bent down with the weight of European **tithes** and taxation, here throw off the load, and stand erect in freedom."

Samuel Goodrich, 1841

Goodrich thought that people who risked everything searching for a better life would make the most of that opportunity once they arrived in America.

Are people encouraged to work harder for their new country if they are enjoying more religious and economic freedom?

The Know-Nothings believed the person in this picture represented the ideal "Native American" citizen at a time when many were suspicious of new immigrants.

immediately banned immigrants from holding any city jobs. But the Know-Nothings faced opposition. In fact, the group was eventually stopped from spreading its influence across Illinois by a 46-year-old state legislator named Abraham Lincoln. The Nativist movement began to crumble soon after.

Now consider *this* ...

The Nativist movement may have collapsed, but its impact it still felt today. Sometimes it seems as if each immigrant group that comes to America feels a little superior to the groups that arrive right after them. ***Why might some form of Nativism be with us today?***

2 Can the U.S. pass a law aimed at people from one country?

By the late 1800s, the nature of immigration in the United States was starting to change. For nearly a century, the nation's "open door" policy toward newcomers had turned out to be its greatest strength. However, as the American West opened up in the 1850s and 1860s, concern grew among many business and political leaders that the "wrong" type of immigrant was entering the country. As newcomers from Asia began to arrive in America in large numbers, a new immigration debate began …

AFFIRMATIVE SIDE

Every new American adds something positive to the U.S. Anyone who has the drive and ambition to gamble everything for a fresh start can make a valuable contribution to the country, no matter who they are or where they come from.

From the Far East to the American West

The discovery of gold in California in the late 1840s started the Gold Rush. Pioneers, prospectors, and homesteaders flocked to the region in the 1850s and 1860s to stake their **claims** and seek their fortunes. Towns and cities sprang up on the west coast, and the building of the nation's transcontinental railroad began. Crossing the rugged U.S. terrain created a great demand for workers. The U.S. alone could not fill this demand. China could help.

As is so often the case with new immigrant groups, the Chinese people were facing challenges at home. Their population was growing rapidly and the country was in the midst of a bloody civil war. These factors convinced many young men to explore other parts of the world. More than a quarter-million Chinese residents came to the American West and found jobs related to the railroad. Some worked for a few years, saved their money, and returned home.

NEGATIVE SIDE

Transportation is now so cheap that anyone can enter the U.S. Certain ethnic groups will take more from America than they contribute. Singling out these people and barring them from entry into the country is a logical measure.

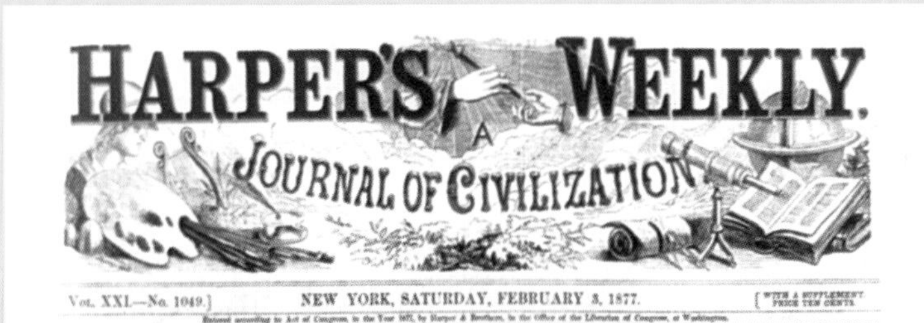

This magazine cover shows immigration officials inspecting Chinese workers arriving in California. Most Chinese immigrants came to America for jobs or to escape unrest in China.

More often, they put down roots in the U.S. Some had no choice—in order to pay for the trip to America, they had to work for many years as laborers at a dollar or two a week.

Almost from the start, the Chinese in America faced hostility and prejudice. They competed with gold and silver prospectors, often taking claims that had been abandoned and finding ways to make them profitable. American workers believed the Chinese were stealing jobs from them because they were willing to work hard for a lower wage. In some western cities—including Los Angeles and San Francisco—anti-Chinese riots led to murders. Some states tried to bar Chinese immigration. However, a treaty between the U.S. and China, signed in 1868, guaranteed free immigration in both directions.

In 1875, Congress passed new **legislation** called the Page Act. It barred entry into the United States for immigrants who were coming to the country as forced labor. It also targeted those who were convicts in their own country.

Make Your Case

"Our courts find it exceedingly difficult to punish criminals among the Chinese unless with the consent of their own authorities. On the other hand, it is believed their secret societies inflict the severest penalties for the infraction of their own regulations."

Horace Davis, 1878

In this speech to Congress, Senator Davis of California claimed that Chinese immigrants often lived together in isolated communities, which allowed them to form their own "government within a government." They countered that this was the only way to escape the prejudice they faced.

Do immigrant groups that purposely isolate themselves pose a threat to the country?

Make Your Case

"If you say that a man shall not come in or shall not become a citizen until he can read and write our language,

or until he can pass an examination upon the Constitution ... you still leave the door open to any man in the world to overcome this and come in. But if you say he shall not have this, that, or the other right because ... he is born in a certain place, I hold that it is a departure from the **republican doctrine**."

Joseph Hawley, 1882

Hawley was a Senator from Connecticut. He felt that it was fair to set minimum standards for people who wanted to come to the U.S. However, he believed it was unfair to deny entry because of a person's birthplace.

What minimum standards are fair and reasonable for new Americans today and in the future?

Although the Page Act did not single out Chinese immigrants, it was aimed directly at them. In 1880, further steps were taken to limit Chinese immigration when the 1868 treaty was renegotiated to greatly favor the U.S. Finally, in 1882, Congress passed the Chinese Exclusion Act. It barred entry to all Chinese laborers. This turned a wave of immigration from that country into a tiny trickle. Two years later, the law was extended to bar Chinese-Americans who had returned to their homeland to conduct business or make family visits. Later changes to the Chinese Exclusion Act required Chinese Americans to carry identification proving their U.S. residency. Without these papers, they could be arrested and deported.

Now consider *this* ...

The Chinese Exclusion Act was the first federal law preventing one specific group from entering the U.S. It was enacted under intense pressure from American workers. They feared competition from low-wage workers, even though Chinese often held jobs that most Americans were unwilling to do. Today, some people make a similar argument about immigrants who cross over the Mexican border into the U.S. ***Does an immigrant who is willing to work for lower pay harm or help America?***

Is America a melting pot or a dumping ground?

During the 1800s, America began to think of itself as a melting pot. Despite predictions of the harm newcomers would do, the mixing of people from different countries and faiths gave the nation great diversity and strength. By the end of the century, however, some Americans wondered whether the "ingredients" being mixed into the melting pot were of high enough quality. The immigration debate during this era focused on immigrants pouring into America who were viewed as backward and uneducated ...

AFFIRMATIVE SIDE

Immigrants from places such as Italy and Russia can strengthen America. What they lack in education and sophistication, they make up for with their willingness to work and their ambition to succeed. The country's diversity is its greatest strength.

The Great Wave

Immigration in the U.S. underwent dramatic change in the second half of the 1800s. From 1800 to 1850, the number of new Americans each year rarely totaled more than 100,000 to 200,000. From 1880 to 1900, an average of 1 million immigrants arrived annually. This figure included Europeans who migrated to Canada and then traveled south across the border. This great migration continued until 1914—when travel from Europe was stopped by World War I—and then picked up again when the war ended in 1918.

In 1907, 1.3 million immigrants officially entered the U.S.—the highest one-year total in history until the 1990s. Some of these people were part of familiar groups, such as the Irish, English, Germans, and those from Scandinavian countries. Also included were Southern Europeans and Eastern Europeans, who often came from small towns and villages in countries such as Italy, Greece, Russia (which included much of Poland at the time), and Austria-Hungary (which was one country from 1867 to 1918).

NEGATIVE SIDE

If America wants to become a true world power, it cannot let in people from the most backward countries. They will put stress on overcrowded cities and fail to adjust to the challenges of life in the U.S. Placing strict limits on "undesirable" newcomers is the only way to protect America.

A ship loaded with immigrants docks in New York in the early 1900s. Most new Americans during this time came from Southern Europe and Eastern Europe.

With this wave of new Americans, however, came new concerns. Were they coming to America to improve their lives and contribute to the country's growth? Or, were they simply running away? Many immigrants journeyed to America with few skills, almost no education, and with only a plan to send money home to their families. This created an additional fear: If these workers did not spend their hard-earned dollars in the U.S., some Americans worried the "draining" of money from the economy would trigger a financial panic.

Un-American New Americans

In the period from 1880 to 1920, an increasing number of Americans believed that immigrants had only one thing in mind: to take advantage of what had already been built by the sacrifices of others. This idea took root during the 1890s,

Make Your Case

"It is unwise to depart from the old American tradition and to discriminate for or against any man who desires to come here and become a citizen ... We cannot afford to consider whether he is Catholic or Protestant, Jew or Gentile, whether he is Englishman or Irishman, Frenchman or German, Japanese, Italian, Scandinavian, Slav, or **Magyar**."

► *Theodore Roosevelt, 1905*

Like many politicians, President Roosevelt sometimes had to straddle the line when it came to his views on immigration. So although he supported the existing ban on Chinese immigrants, he welcomed everyone else with open arms.

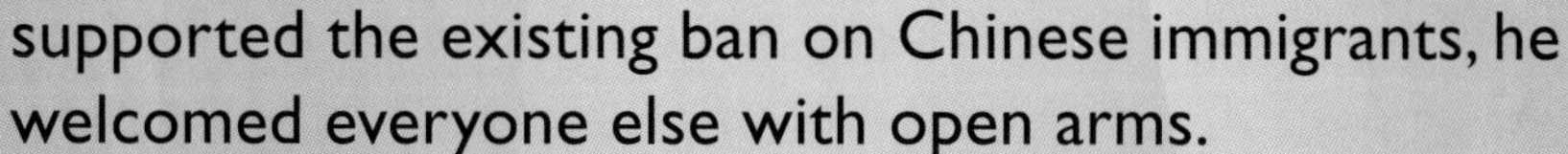

What reasons might Roosevelt have had for taking the position he did?

when several financial calamities shook the nation. America's economic problems were caused mostly by unfair and irresponsible business practices. But many Americans instead blamed the new immigrants, who seemed to be everywhere.

During this time, the idea of keeping certain European immigrants out of America started to gain in popularity. The thinking was that people from England, Germany, and Scandinavia were from free and energetic societies, and therefore they were "good" immigrants. By comparison, Southern Europe, Eastern Europe, Ireland, Latin America, and Asia were considered backwards and downtrodden societies. People from these countries were viewed as "bad" immigrants, with little to offer America.

This argument could be very persuasive. Soon, groups began to pressure the government into making changes. In 1907, the U.S. Immigration Commission was formed to study the recent wave of immigrants coming to American shores. The commission was made up of respected congressmen and senators. In 1911, they issued a report that seemed to prove everyone's suspicions. It claimed that immigrants from Eastern

Make Your Case

"Although transplanted into a new environment, living in abnormal conditions in industrial centers, and meeting more temptations in a week than they would in a lifetime in rural communities in their homeland, when their criminal record is compared with that of the native-born males, it comes out better than even."

Peter Roberts, 1911

Roberts wrote a book called *The New Immigration*. In it he showed that most of the immigrants in the early 1900s came from farm communities, not the crime-ridden and overcrowded cities of Europe.

Why was it important for supporters of immigration to emphasize that most new Americans were from farms and not cities?

Europe and Southern Europe posed a great threat to American culture. The 1911 report convinced most Americans that something needed to be done about immigration.

In 1921, Congress passed the Emergency Immigration Act. It set **quotas** on immigration from each nation based on the 1910 U.S. census. This dramatically reduced the number of immigrants that would be allowed from places such as Italy, Russia, and Hungary. An even stricter immigration act was passed in 1924. It reversed the quota back to the 1890 standard. One effect of the 1924 law was that it prevented future entry into the U.S. to large numbers of Jewish people. This would lead to one of history's great humanitarian catastrophes.

Now consider *this* ...

The immigration laws of the 1920s put the government's stamp of approval on the idea that certain immigrants were better than others. Thousands of people trying to come to the U.S. were turned away. America went through a brief period of prosperity during the 1920s, followed by a crushing financial collapse—the Great Depression—which lasted until World War II. ***How might cutting off an important source of cheap and willing immigrant labor have contributed to the country's economic struggles?***

4 Does America have a responsibility to offer freedom to others?

After the new laws of the 1920s went into effect, immigration to the United States dropped dramatically. During the 1930s, when America found itself in the grip of the Great Depression, immigration slowed to just over 50,000 people a year. That number dropped even lower after World War II began. At the same time, new governments came to power in Europe that discriminated against certain ethnic and religious groups. The debate now centered on whether the U.S. had an obligation to bend the rules and let people in when it was a matter of life and death …

AFFIRMATIVE SIDE

Welcoming people who have been denied basic human rights in their own countries is exactly what America stands for. This is how a great society is created. Our commitment to fight for freedom should start at home.

The Door Slammed Shut

The limits and quotas created by the immigration laws of 1921 and 1924 prevented millions from coming to the U.S. As in decades past, many of these people cast their eyes on America, hoping for a chance at a better life. However, during the 1930s and 1940s, more and more people saw passage to America as a way to *stay alive*. Among the groups most affected by the new immigration policies were Jewish people from Europe. Only 100,000 were allowed into the U.S. during the 1930s, despite the fact that they were being persecuted in Germany and other countries.

In 1939, a ship carrying more than 900 Jewish refugees from Germany was denied permission to land in Florida. The ship was sent back to Europe, where more than half of the passengers died in the Holocaust. After news of the death camps reached the U.S. government, some politicians still worked to keep Jewish people from entering the country.

NEGATIVE SIDE

When America is at its weakest, a strict immigration policy keeps the country strong. In the years between World War I and World War II, immigration law prohibited foreign **radicals** *and enemy spies from entering the country—and helped the U.S. survive the Great Depression.*

Refugees prepare to board the General Black. The ship was the first to bring displaced persons to the U.S. when immigration laws changed after World War II.

In the late 1940s, after Americans became aware of the horrors of the concentration camps, attitudes on immigration began to change.

What About Refugees?

Although the old laws stayed on the books, the government began to create "loopholes" through which immi-

Make Your Case

"It is the duty of all *Americans* ... [to] unite in an effort to reduce immigration to the lowest possible point or stop it altogether, and to compel the foreigners now here either to accept our traditions and ideals or else to return to the land from which they came, by deportation or otherwise."

Madison Grant, 1933

Grant was an influential conservationist who worked to save several animal species from extinction. He believed America would go extinct unless immigrants were either turned away or forced to abandon their national customs and cultures.

Does it make a country stronger when everyone looks, acts, and sounds the same?

grants could enter the country. For example, women who married or became engaged to American soldiers were welcomed into the U.S. as citizens, thanks to the War Brides Act. After that, their families could follow them to the U.S.

A trickier subject was what to do with people fleeing Communist governments in the aftermath of World War II. The Soviet Union (a group of countries that was led by current-day Russia) controlled almost all of Eastern Europe after the war ended. The Soviets imposed **Communism**, a form of government that America considered extremely hostile to its safety and values. The U.S. encouraged people to oppose Communism and to try to escape from those countries that embraced it. But this philosophy also meant that America had a responsibility to accept these political refugees. The same was true for people who survived wartime prison camps and others whose homes had been destroyed by fighting and bombing.

The American people began putting pressure on the government to lift the old immigration restrictions. The most vocal were typically the children and grandchildren of Europeans who came to the U.S. in the 1800s and early 1900s. They were Americans, to be sure, but they had deep affection and concern for friends and family who were struggling overseas.

Make Your Case

"I have analyzed closely the bill which was sent to me for signature. Its good points can be stated all too briefly ... The bad points of the bill are numerous."

Harry S. Truman, 1948

President Truman supported the Displaced Persons Act of 1948. It enabled more than 200,000 refugees to come to the U.S. But Truman thought the legislation was far from perfect. He felt it discriminated against Jewish and Catholic people.

Why would Truman have signed off on a bill with which he was so unhappy?

In 1948, Congress passed the Displaced Persons Act. For a limited period of time, it allowed certain groups of Europeans to gain full citizenship in the U.S. Almost immediately, more than 200,000 refugees were admitted to the country.

Over the next 15 years, new loopholes were created in response to humanitarian crises or political upheaval. For example, in the early 1960s, Fidel Castro imposed a Communist government on Cuba. Much of that nation's middle class was branded "enemies of the revolution." More than 400,000 Cubans fled to the U.S. in the years that followed. In 1980, the United States passed the Refugee Act. This created a permanent set of rules for dealing with people who were driven out of their own countries.

Now consider *this* ...

The lessons learned before and after World War II showed that strict immigration policies did not always have the intended effect. Also, they did not cover extraordinary events. In the years since, the U.S. has launched wars against countries led by dictators and leaders who limit the freedom of the citizens they rule. ***Does the U.S. have a responsibility to offer citizenship to people who are fleeing their own countries in pursuit of freedom in America?***

Can a multicultural country be a strong country?

During the 1950s and 1960s, two forces changed attitudes toward immigration. First, America tried to expand its economic and political influence throughout the world. Second, the **Civil Rights** movement in America showed the importance of valuing the skills and heritage of all people, not just those with white skin. Unlike past groups, the immigrants entering the United States after 1965 were reluctant to abandon the languages and cultures of their homelands. This brought about a new debate over whether "too much" diversity was a good thing …

AFFIRMATIVE SIDE

What will give the U.S. life and strength in the future is its willingness to make room for everyone. For the nation to maintain its position as an international power, it will need a better understanding of the world. What better place to gain that understanding than from the multicultural makeup of its own people?

Times Change

After six decades of strict limits on immigration, the U.S. reopened its doors to the entire world in the 1960s. The Immigration and Nationality Act of 1965 erased or greatly reduced the old quotas. The most important part of the new law was the creation of a new category of immigrant. Anyone who was an immediate relative of a U.S. citizen now had a legal path to citizenship. This created a "chain" of immigration that might start with one family member gaining citizenship. That person could then be joined by his or her family members. The changes in immigration law during the 1960s triggered an explosion of diversity in the United States. Within a couple of generations, the "face" of America looked very different than it had for almost three centuries.

The most noticeable change in immigration after 1965 was the wave of new Americans arriving from Asia. This was especially true of those from the Philippines and South Korea.

NEGATIVE SIDE

One of the cornerstones of America's success has been a common language and culture. To enjoy the full benefits of citizenship, new Americans should follow the lead of every past immigrant group and work to blend in. Too much diversity will fragment a society that works best when everyone works together.

Make Your Case

"My hope is that I will take the good from my experiences and **extrapolate** them further into areas with which I am unfamiliar. I accept there will be some based on my gender and my Latina heritage."

Sonia Sotomayor (hand raised), 2009

Sotomayor became the U.S. Supreme Court's first Latina Justice in 2009. Her parents grew up in Puerto Rico, and she admitted that her family's background affects the way she thinks.

How much influence should the family history of judges have on the way they make court decisions?

To a lesser degree, there was also an increase in immigrants from Pakistan, India, China, Hong Kong, Taiwan, Japan, and the Middle East. Along with these people came millions from the Caribbean and Latin America, and also a growing number of immigrants from Africa.

In almost all of these cases, the driving force to come to America was economic. There were many countries around the world that tended to have rapidly growing populations, low wages, and poor **social services**. For example, in Mexico, the population had increased from fewer than 15 million in 1900 to more than 100 million by 2000. For many Mexicans, the best chance for a good life lay across the U.S. border. Some entered the country legally, but others did not. Illegal immigrants from South America and Central America also entered the U.S. through Mexico.

What About that Border?

Securing America's borders to prevent illegal immigration has been an issue since the 1950s. At that time, a program was started to round up illegal aliens and deport them.

Make Your Case

"Real reform means establishing a responsible pathway to earned citizenship—a path that includes passing a background check, paying taxes and a meaningful penalty, learning English, and going to the back of the line behind the folks trying to come here legally."

Barack Obama, 2013

In his 2013 State of the Union speech, President Obama made immigration reform one of the key issues of his second term in office. He believed that nearly every immigrant should have a path to citizenship.

Is it fair to make people living in the U.S. illegally wait longer for citizenship than people living in other countries?

Walls have been constructed along some parts of the United States-Mexico border. This one was built in Arizona in 2011.

This involved house-to-house searches in Mexican-American neighborhoods and random stops of people who "looked Mexican." These tactics and others like them violated civil rights—and led to the end of the program soon after it began.

From the 1960s right into the 21st century, the number of Spanish-speaking immigrants (both legal and illegal) in the U.S. grew largely unchecked. Today, Hispanics make up the country's largest non-white ethnic group, numbering more than 50 million. At first, most families tended to live in **insulated** neighborhoods. But after a generation or two, they started to blend their cultures and languages into everyday American life.

This growth did not come without problems. The U.S. shares a border with Mexico that stretches almost 2,000 miles from the Pacific Ocean to the Gulf of Mexico. It is just about impossible to prevent people from crossing that border and entering the country. When people are caught living in the U.S. illegally, they are deported to their countries of origin. However, there is little to stop them from reentering the United States. In 2010, more than 10 million people were believed to be living in the U.S. illegally; most were from Mexico or Central America.

Can this illegal immigration be halted? Some have suggested that a wall be constructed along the entire border. However, building a wall would be expensive, and it would still be possible to climb over. And what about the millions already living in the U.S. illegally? How can you throw 10 million people out of the country at the same time?

It would not only be impossible, it might create a problem much worse. As with previous immigrant groups, these new Americans do the jobs that most people in the U.S. are unwilling or unable to do. They are an important part of the economy. By some estimates, they contribute two dollars worth of value for every dollar they use in social services.

Now consider *this* ...

In 2008, Barack Obama won the U.S. presidential election. People around the world applauded the fact that the nation had made a person of color its new leader. They also recognized that strong support from immigrant groups helped him win the election. ***How much of an impact did the Immigration and Nationality Act of 1965 have on Obama's victory 43 years later?***

6 Find your voice

In recent years, three issues have been at the center of the debate surrounding new Americans. These are complicated questions that invite many points of view. Much like the immigration debates over the last 200 years, they involve economics, politics, powerful fears, and strong emotions. There is a very good chance that people will be debating these issues throughout your lifetime.

More than ever before, young people from Spanish-speaking cultures are making themselves heard in America.

1 Should people who have been been living in the U.S. illegally be allowed to become citizens sooner than those who have followed the rules?

If it were simply a matter of fairness, the answer would be *No*. After all, why should people who have broken the rules be given an advantage over people who officially apply for citizenship? The problem is that there are more than 10 million people living in the U.S. illegally. As discussed in the previous chapter, they provide important services and help the economy through their work. What would happen if all of them were told to leave the country? More to the point, how do you *make* 10 million people leave the country? It would take many thousands of new immigration agents and law enforcement workers—and the government cannot afford that. This is why politicians debate different "pathways to citizenship" that solve this problem in a positive way.

When debating pathways to citizenship, some point out that the U.S. has always been a nation of immigrants.

Should a child who grew up in the U.S. be deported as an adult?

In 2001, a new law was proposed that attempted to answer this question. It was called Development, Relief, and Education for Alien Minors—or the DREAM Act, for short. It proposed that people who came to the U.S. with their families illegally as a child or young teenager could become citizens if they fulfilled certain requirements. These requirements include graduating from high school and showing they are of good moral character. Those who support this type of law say that children should not be punished (denied the rights of a citizen or be deported) for a "crime" they did not commit. Those who oppose this type of law say it encourages families with young children to enter the U.S. illegally, and that it might also be used to shield gang members who came to America as children.

Should the U.S. do more to encourage foreign students to become new Americans?

Right now, foreign students educated at American colleges and universities are not allowed to stay and become citizens after completing their studies. The **student visas** that enable them to attend school in the U.S. push them out of the coun-

Protests demanding immigration reform such as this one have become commonplace in the U.S.

try as soon as they earn their diplomas. Many would prefer to stay and work for American companies. Can the country afford to educate these young minds, only to send them home? Wouldn't these people make the best new Americans?

All the issues in this chapter are being discussed right now as part of immigration reform—the push to change policies that determine who can become a new American. As with immigration laws throughout history, change takes place over time. Now is the time to join the national conversation on immigration. Think about these issues and consider both sides of these debates. Where do you stand? One day soon—through the candidates you support, the dollars you spend, and your own personal feelings about immigration—you will have a voice!

7 Point — Counterpoint

America's policy on immigration has been greatly influenced by public opinion over the years. That opinion is shaped by many factors, including personal experience, common sense, and what others write or have to say. We think about the different sides of an issue. We look at how it affects us, our family members, and our friends. We consider the best solutions. And we weigh what the smartest and most influential people believe.

This was true in the 1700s and 1800s, when Americans got their information from pamphlets, newspapers, and speeches. It was true in the 1900s, when radio and television brought ideas to an even wider audience. It remains true today, as we scan websites, blogs, and social media. The voices in this chapter have helped shape the debate on immigration. The words may be a little different, but the passion behind them would fit in any era …

Point — Counterpoint

"America is open to receive not only the **opulent** and respectable stranger, but the oppressed and persecuted of all nations and religions, whom we shall welcome to participate in all of our rights and privileges, if by decency and **propriety of conduct** they appear to merit the enjoyment."

George Washington, 1783

"Why should Pennsylvania, founded by the English, become a colony of aliens, who will shortly be so numerous as to Germanize us instead of us Anglifying them, and will never adopt our language or customs, any more than they can acquire our complexion?"

Benjamin Franklin, 1751

In the days of our founding fathers, people were already debating who should be allowed to become an American. Franklin felt immigrants threatened the colonists' way of life. Washington believed we should open our doors to newcomers.

Why was the issue of immigration policy so important in the early days of America?

Point — Counterpoint

"Continual emigration, and a constant mixing of the blood of different races, is highly conducive to physical and mental superiority." *Thomas L. Nichols, 1845*

"Had they foreseen the vast, the appalling increase in immigration upon us at present, there can be no reasonable doubt that laws to **naturalize** the foreigners and to give up to them the country, its liberties, its destiny, would not have been authorized by the Constitution."
Garrett Davis (right), 1849

Nichols was a medical doctor and historian. He celebrated the diversity that immigrants brought to American shores. Davis, a Senator from Kentucky, argued that our founding fathers would have made laws against immigrants had they foreseen the millions who poured into the U.S. during the 19th century.

In what ways does diversity make America stronger?

Point — Counterpoint

"Why was I doing it? Because I wanted to survive. I wanted to live. I wanted to learn what it means to be an American."
Jose Antonio Vargas, 2011

"Hospitals are closing across the country … and college students find that summer jobs have dried up due to illegal immigration, and wages across the board are depressed by the overwhelming influx of cheap and illegal labor."
Elton Gallegly, 2010

Gallegly represented California in the U.S. House of Representatives. He pointed out the costs created by illegal immigration. Vargas, a prize-winning reporter, revealed that he had entered the U.S. illegally at the age of 12 with his family.

Do illegal immigrants do more harm than good when they come to the United States?

There has never been a better time to make your voice heard. No matter which side of an issue you take, remember that a debate doesn't have to be an argument. If you enjoy proving your point, join your school's debate team. If your school doesn't have one, find a teacher who will serve as coach and get more students involved. If you want to make a real splash, email the people who represent you in government. If they don't listen now, they may hear from you later … in the voting booth!

GLOSSARY

Civil Rights — The rights of citizens to freedom and equality.

Claims — Pieces of land that are mined.

Communism — A system of commerce and government that outlaws private ownership and encourages people to share equally in work and reward.

Extrapolate — Extend what you know to something unknown.

Federal — Related to a government that can make laws for a group of states.

Injurious — Likely to cause damage or harm.

Insulated — Protected from outside elements.

Legislation — A group of laws.

Magyar — An ethnic Hungarian.

Naturalize — Admit for citizenship.

Opulent — Wealthy or rich-looking.

Propriety of Conduct — Good behavior.

Protestant — A member of a Christian faith that is separate from Catholicism. Protestant churches include Presbyterians, Lutherans, and Baptists.

Quotas — Limits or fixed numbers.

Radicals — People who want to make big, controversial changes.

Rationale — Reasons for a course of action.

Republican Doctrine — Beliefs that support the idea of a republic.

Social Services — Benefits supplied by a government.

Student Visas — Special permits that allow foreigners to study in the U.S.

Tithes — A portion of income pledged to a church.

Sources

The authors relied on many different sources for their information. Listed below are some of their primary sources:

A Nation by Design. Aristede R. Zolberg. Cambridge, Massachusetts. Harvard University Press, 2008.

Coming to America: A History of Immigration and Ethnicity in American Life. Roger Daniels. New York, New York. Harper Perennial, 2002.

Debating Immigration. Carol M Swain, Editor. New York, New York. Cambridge University Press, 2007.

Guarding the Golden Door: American Immigration Policy and Immigrants since 1882. Roger Daniels. New York, New York. Hill and Wang, 2004.

Turning Points in World History: Immigration. Jeff Hay, Editor. Farmington Hills, Michigan. Greenhaven Press, 2001.

Resources

For more information on the subjects covered in this book, consider starting with these books and websites:

Encyclopedia of North American Immigration. John Powell. New York, New York. Facts on File, 2005.

Facts About American Immigration. David M. Brownstone & Irene M. H. Franck. New York, New York. W. Wilson, 2001.

The New York Times
www.nytimes.com
http://learning.blogs.nytimes.com/2010/04/27/learning-about-u-s-immigration-with-the-new-york-times/

Library of Congress
www.loc.gov
Search for Immigration on this site!

INDEX

Page numbers in **bold** refer to illustrations.

AUTHORS

GEOFFREY C. HARRISON and **THOMAS F. SCOTT** are educators at the Rumson Country Day School, a K thru 8 school in Rumson, New Jersey. Mr. Harrison is the head of the math department and coordinator of the school's forensics team. Mr. Scott has been teaching upper school history at RCDS for more than 25 years and is head of that department. They enjoy nothing more than a great debate … just ask their students!